W9-BDC-899

BEARS ON THE BRAIN

by Lucille Recht Penner
illustrated by Lynn Adams

Kane Press, Inc.
New York

To Oscar and Gabriel Escobar—L.R.P.

Acknowledgement: Our thanks to Vivian VanPeenen, Curator of Education, Reid Park Zoo, Tucson, AZ for helping us make this book as accurate as possible.

Copyright © 2003 by Kane Press, Inc.

All rights reserved. No part of this book may be reproduced or transmitted in any form or by any means, electronic or mechanical, including photocopying, recording, or by any information storage and retrieval system, without permission in writing from the publisher. For information regarding permission, contact the publisher through its website: www.kanepress.com.

Library of Congress Cataloging-in-Publication Data

Penner, Lucille Recht.
Bears on the brain / by Lucille Penner ; illustrated by Lynn Adams.
p. cm. — (Science solves it!)
Summary: Something has been making tracks in Oscar's back yard and eating his mother's red flowers, so Oscar and his friends devise a plan to get a clearer set of prints and compare them to pictures in a library book.
ISBN: 978-1-57565-121-7 (alk. paper)
[1. Animal tracks—Fiction.] I. Adams, Lynn, ill. II. Title. III. Series.
PZ7.P38465 Be 2003
[Fic]—dc21

2002010327

10 9 8 7 6 5

First published in the United States of America in 2003 by Kane Press, Inc.
Printed in U.S.A.

Science Solves It! is a registered trademark of Kane Press, Inc.

Book Design/Art Direction: Edward Miller

www.kanepress.com

Gabriel, Sam, and I were spending the weekend at Oscar's. Sam's a girl. So am I. My name is Jill. We were playing Clue in the clubhouse. Oscar had just left to get some snacks.

"Help! Help!" It was Oscar.

We raced outside.

Oscar's little brother, Henry, came running. "What is it?" he yelled.

"A *bear*!" Oscar shrieked.

We all looked around. "There's no bear here," we told him.

"But it *was* here!" Oscar said. "Look at those tracks!"

"Those tracks are pretty small," Sam said.

"So, it was a *small* bear!" Oscar said.

Big or small, bears scare Oscar. You know the commercial where a bear is driving a car? Oscar can't watch it.

"It gives me a stomachache," Oscar says.

"There's no bear here now," I said.

"Good," Henry said. He went back inside.

A minute later Oscar's mom called out from the garden. "Something is eating my beautiful red flowers! Have you kids seen any strange animals around?"

"No," I said. "But we saw animal tracks."

Oscar's mom shook her head. "We didn't have problems like this in the city," she said.

"Don't worry—we'll figure it out," I said.

But it wasn't that easy.

Oscar was sure it was a bear.

Gabriel didn't agree. "A bear would have eaten *all* the flowers," he said. "Not just a few."

"Not if it was in a hurry to get to the banana peels and pizza crusts," Oscar said.

"Maybe it was a cat," I said.

"No way," said Sam. "A cat couldn't knock over that big garbage can."

"Mac could," Gabriel said. Mac is Oscar's dog.

"He would *never* do that," Oscar said. "Anyway, he was inside all night."

"Stop! I can't think anymore," Sam said. "I'm too hungry."

Oscar jumped up. "I forgot to get the snacks!" He ran into his house.

Oscar came back with four juice boxes and a giant bag. "Yum. Crunchy Triple Cheeze Bits. My favorite," said Sam.

For a while, no one spoke. We were too busy munching and thinking. Everyone had a different idea about the mystery animal.

"The only real clue we have are the tracks that Oscar found," I said. "We've got to find out more about animal tracks."

We finished the Cheeze Bits and headed for the library.

We were lucky. We found a huge book on animal tracks. "There must be hundreds in here," said Gabriel.

"What about these raccoon tracks?" I asked.

"I'm not sure they're the same as the tracks in Oscar's yard," said Sam.

Gabriel thought the mystery animal might be a deer. But deer tracks looked like upside-down hearts. Not a bit like ours.

"Maybe it's a skunk," said Sam.

"Nah," we all said.

"Let's check out the book," I said. "Then we can compare the pictures to the real tracks."

I went and stood in line.

"Wait a minute!" Oscar called. "I found a website and printed out some bear tracks."

"Oscar," I said, "you have bears on the brain."

We looked at the tracks as soon as we got back. But they were a mess.

"Looks like a bird walked in them," said Gabriel.

"We can't tell anything from these," Sam said.

“I have a great idea!” I said. “Let’s pour flour around. If the animal walks in it, the tracks will be really clear! We can keep watch and see what happens.”

“Why do we need flour if we’re going to watch?” Gabriel asked.

"It might be too dark to see," I said. "This way we have two chances. If we don't see the animal, we'll see its tracks in the flour!"

"That's a great idea," Oscar said.

"Time for dinner, kids!" It was Oscar's mom, calling from the kitchen.

"Just in time," said Sam. "I was getting hungry."

Dinner was barbecued chicken. Yum! We hoped the mystery animal liked chicken.

After dinner we played Go Fish with Henry.

Then we got out our sleeping bags and stuff. Oscar got a big bag of flour.

We spread the flour all around the garbage can and near the red flowers. I made a footprint to see if my idea would work. It came out great!

"Okay, flower-eating garbage-picker," Sam yelled. "We're ready for you!"

"What if we all fall asleep?" I said.

"Won't happen," Gabriel told me. "I'm sleeping with my hockey helmet on. No one can sleep with a hockey helmet on."

"I'm wearing my itchy King Kong outfit," Oscar said. "I'll be awake all night scratching."

ALL ABOUT ANIMAL TRACKS

“I’m keeping my hair in braids,” Sam said. “I can never sleep in braids. What about you, Jill?”

I got on the exercise bike. “I’ll pedal until morning,” I said.

Guess what? We all fell asleep.

I woke up first. "Hey," I shouted. "It's morning already!"

Everyone ran outside to look for tracks in the flour.

“It worked!” I said.

“Was it a bear?” Oscar asked.

Sam was looking at the pictures. “It’s a raccoon!” she said.

Gabriel measured the tracks. “Front paws two inches,” he said. “It’s a raccoon all right.”

"Wait a minute. What's that?" I pointed at a small sneaker track near the flowers.

"It must be Henry's," Oscar said.

Just then Henry came around the corner. He was carrying a bag full of flowers—red flowers.

"These are for my teacher," he said. "I picked them. I like her, and she likes red flowers."

"Aha!" I said. "We've solved *two* mysteries!"

Oscar's Mom came to the door. "Oh, no," she moaned. "My beautiful red flowers."

"Sorry, Mom," Henry said. He told her why he had picked them. "I won't ever do it again," he promised.

"I know you won't," she said. She gave him a hug.

Then we told her how we'd proved that a raccoon had been messing with the garbage.

"So I guess I'll just get raccoon-proof garbage cans!" she said. "Let's celebrate with a special breakfast—blueberry pancakes!"

We were just taking our first bites when a news bulletin came on.

"A bear escaped from the zoo," the announcer said. "But it was caught early this morning. It smelled of barbecue sauce. And its feet were covered in some strange white stuff. No one can figure out what it is."

"Ha!" Oscar said. "I *knew* it was a bear."

"But they *are* raccoon tracks," Sam insisted. "We even measured them."

Oscar didn't hear her. He was outside.

We ran after him and started looking for bear tracks. All we saw were raccoon tracks.

Then Oscar bent down and picked up the garbage-can lid. He jumped back.

"I told you!" he shouted.

Oscar took the picture of the bear tracks out of his pocket. It was a perfect match.

"So," I said slowly, "Oscar was right. A bear really *was* here!"

We all stared at one another.

Yikes!

THINK LIKE A SCIENTIST

Jill and her friends think like scientists—and so can you!

When scientists compare things, they tell how they are alike and how they are different. Sometimes they put them side-by-side and compare shape and size. Sometimes they use measuring tools and compare measurements.

Look Back

Compare the skunk tracks on page 13 to the raccoon tracks on page 12. How are they the same? How are they different? On page 23, what does Sam compare the tracks to? How does Gabriel check to see if Sam is right?

Try This!

You and your friend can compare footprints!
You will need:

- 2 shoebox lids
- sand or flour
- a ruler

Fill each lid with sand or flour. Press your bare foot into the sand in one lid. Have your friend do the same in the other lid. Now compare your footprints. Look at the shape. Measure the size with the ruler. How are your footprints the same? How are they different?

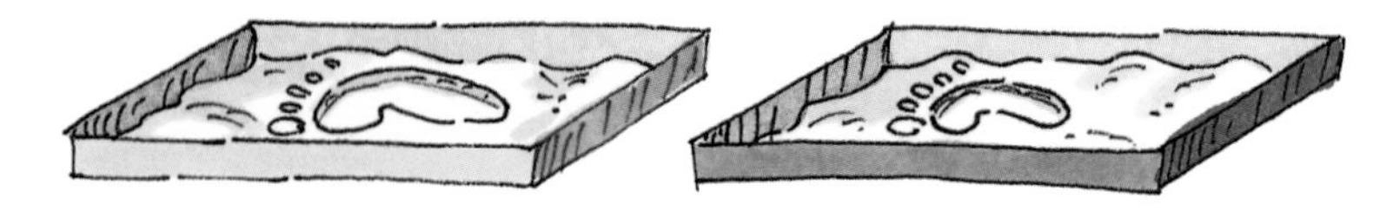